A Hungry Wolf on the Prowl

The Family that Preys Together Stays Together

Chapter 1

In a dark, shady corner of the city sits a night club that caters to the who's who of the known and unknown of the underworld and VIPs of the rich and infamous, only if you are in the know will you be admitted.

Club Vibe is the place to be, a dark dank musty building with 4 floors surrounding the dance floor. Each floor with a bar and bathrooms with silver and gold trimming, for the adventurous a pole runs from the top floor down to the first floor, only the greatest talented dancers ever slide, gyrate and caress on the pole. The regular dancers stick to the dance floor and the chair dancers stick to their tables. The watchers stick to the rails on each floor to watch the dancers on the floor and flock to see the great polers work and soar on the pole.

Smoke fills the club and lights alternate with varying colors to the sound of the music that thumps from the DJ's booth.

At the back of the club is a door that leads to a dark hallway with rooms on either side, but only the true members are allowed to enter here, the door is guarded by several security people that are not bouncers and part of the security of Club Vibe.

There are no cameras and phones allowed beyond the door and all members and guests have been vetted and signed

Non-Disclosure Agreements and waivers to participate in any activity in any room. IE, what happens here stays here.

This is what the Members of the Den must go through, and the regular club goers do not know that this door exists and never see any Den Members arriving or leaving.

Dante York, a young entrepreneur in the city that makes deals everyday buying and selling property and business entities and known for hosting bodacious lavish fetish parties is arriving at Club Vibe, he is surrounded by his entourage and hot groupies that love to show off on the floors and move about the club trying to impress the other club goers.

Only a select few of the entourage know that Dante is a Den Member.

One by one they disappear from the larger group and find their way back to the Den.

KyRel Dukes, Dante's right hand man and his best friend since grade school is the last to enter. He enters the Blue room and sees a couple of Den Members he is familiar with. He makes his way over to them making sure that he acknowledges everyone while casually meandering over to the couple. Taking note of the large couches and large beds in the room.

KyRel! The gentleman says while signaling his wife to come over closer.

"How have you been my dear young fellow? Any more deals to be made today or are you and Dante done doing business?"

He says with a laugh of a wealthy person from old money.

"Business is always being conducted no matter the time, place or event or affair Wellington."

KyRel responds with a slight chuckle, while surveying the room.

Wellington Stetson McCoy Garrison V is a legacy Den Member, he is the owner of several buildings in the city and the biggest investment banker in the state. His great great grandfather was the founder of the Den. He is the one who the movers and shakers and elite Den Members go to for news and contacts for deals and controls all infractions that occur in the Den and has final say over who is in and who is out.

"I hope you remember the rules." Wellington says, with a sly smile.

"I do." KyRel says while pretending to not notice Wellington's wife as she is drawing closer to them.

"Well, I hope you enjoy your time here and do partake of everything that is offered and consider every deal proposed with vigorous zeal with your vire straight and true. He begins to meander off and make small talk with other Members with his wife in tow."

As KyRel is ordering a drink at the bar, Dante comes over and asks how the chat was with the old stiff.

"He is the same as he always is, an old rich dick of a bastard that has a hot young wife because of his money and name. I wonder if he has Viagra stock and gets his heart pills confused with the Viagra, wife number 3 must enjoy that wrinkly old tater tot dick."

Dante laughs and sips from his drink and almost chokes when he notices the news report scroll on the television.

"Oh My God, I knew her in college, he lets out a sigh, I never could get her in my bed or anywhere for that matter."

KyRel turns to see the scroll mentioning that a local office building had been destroyed and the main tenant of the building, Rose Farkas was missing.

"With so many to choose from and that you have had how did you fail to land that?"

"It was way too difficult; she was a virgin and had daddy issues."

"Seems like she was into some deep shit, that is stuff that the cartel does."

"I don't know man, I lost contact with her after graduation and had other conquests to bag and bed."

"Just like in here, several have been asking about you, awaiting the arrival of the almighty sex god Dante."

Dante laughs while making eye contact with a young Den Member who has been watching the two friends banter with each other. He gives a nod to the young man to come over and tells KyRel to prepare for a shark attack.

The young Den Member saunters over and immediately begins to pepper the men with questions ranging from how they are members and if they could land him a meeting with Wellington.

"Whoa there fella." Dante says with a slight hand wave.

"You do know that there are rules and protocols that must be met?"

The young Member looks aghast and did not realize he had committed a faux pa.

"Pardon me sir, it is my first adventure into this soiree, and I have briefly read up on the rules, would you be as kind to bring me abreast of them."

"KyRel? Should we let this young lion be a part of our little party or allow him to flounder in the deep?"

"Let him flounder and drown and then revive him with the life waters of the Den."

"You are surely jesting, or am I that poorly of a prime candidate?"

"He is only joking with you lad, or as you say jesting."

"First off fella you need to learn rule number one. Do not approach other Members without being properly introduced to them and not having at least 2 interactions. So, you should have had the attendant walk you over to us and make proper introductions. Rule number 2 do not ask questions until you have been to at least one event. Rule number 3 business is not conducted until you have attended 2 events, you are only allowed to watch and not stay at one couch or bed too long. Rule number 4 never get involved with any business being conducted without being asked. And finally, Rule number 5 no deal is confirmed final until all parties have been satisfied and thoroughly and completely reached an agreement of completion.

Now with that walk your ass back over to the attendant and have them come make the proper introductions and then take your ass around the room and make proper introductions with everyone and then you pay attention and watch everything that happens."

The young Member saunters back to the door with his head low and then returns to the guys with the attendant who introduces them and then they acknowledge the young Member as a Member and allows him to count this as interaction number one.

They then turn their attention to the couch against the north wall and begin to head over and start to conduct business with a pair of ladies that have undressed and announced that they are open to receive and negotiate with all that are able to entertain a joint venture.

A bell rings and masked people walk around the Members taking slips of papers over to the two ladies, they look at them one by one and whisper to each other without looking at the Members. Dante takes note of the young Member who he now knows as Marcus Willoughby, the heir to the Willoughby Steel Company and Willoughby Construction Company. A vast family of business leaders from Steel to Finance and Manufacturing all around the world. Young Marcus' father is known to be shrewd and calculating and a very pious and devoted Christian man and his mother just as devout as her husband. What would they say if they knew their son was galivanting around town in night clubs, hobnobbing with shady characters and a Member of the Den, the most secret and elite sex club in the state?

KyRel also has taken note and leans over to Dante, appears that our new acquaintance is beginning to figure out how business is conducted, what do you think he will do when the trade bell rings?

"I figure he will hold his dick a bit and then must excuse himself to the bathroom."

"No, KyRel, he will be more astute and try to worm his way into the trade engaging in breaking the rules again, because he comes from such a Chaste and Christian family."

Marcus is now appearing to notice that the slips of papers contain numbers, wondering if the numbers represent money or another form of bidding, he turns to the guys, and they allow him to approach.

"Gentlemen, may I be as so bold as to hazard a guess about the slips that I see?"

"Look fella if you must hazard then you have not been paying attention. The numbers do not represent money nor are they a bank account, they are the measurements, height, weight and length of male Members and breasts, waists, and hips of female Members."

KyRel chimes in. "The ladies will decide if they are keen to take on one Member each or multiple Members together and the winning measurements will be escorted to the couch and the trade bell will ring to commence the trade and business will be conducted and we will move to an appropriate distance not to interrupt and watch as for as long as you like or until the business deal is completed, you are free to roam about the room and seeing is this is now our second interaction you are now free to talk and conduct real business with us."

"Oh, now that is a splendid idea, but I think I will watch the business at hand for a while and get the lay of the land so to speak."

"Marcus you are indeed a remarkable Member. Most new members would have been holding their milk and excused themselves to the bathroom by now. And you have cost me $1000 and one of my favorite ladies in the Orange room to Dante."

KyRel is only being kind in front of Marcus, but he is a sore loser and has always been a loser to Dante throughout their lives. A situation that is becoming volatile day by day but unnoticed by anyone.

Anyone except for the lurker who is maintaining an eye on the two friends, and no one has noticed entered the Den and following the friends at close length.

Dante and KyRel exit the Blue room making their way into the Orange room where they are greeted by a bevy of bodacious women scantily clad in sheer black robes and heels and handed cocktails called the Summer Sunset, the only drink that is allowed in the Orange room. It is made with 4 ounces of Orange Juice, 2 ounces of Pineapple juice and ounce of Mango juice with 2 shots of vodka, a drop of honey and a splash of grenadine and served with 2 red B12 vitamins.

On the orange couch across the room business is being conducted by 6 Members who are so enthralled and entangled with each other, that they have not noticed a crowd forming, business is thoroughly being completed and each Member is appearing to satisfactorily meet the conditions of the deal. One female Member has her ass being licked and her pussy licked while giving a male Member head as he is licking another female Member and she is licking the pussy of the Member that is licking the other Member's ass and this ball of oral and anal licking is permeating the room.

On the other side of the room on the orange bed are a pair of muscular men that the guys recognize as the Harrison twins, they had long known these rich bastards since freshmen year of college and had a long-standing rivalry. On the bed with them were two Members whos' husbands did not seem to mind that the ladies were being treated to such a workover by the twins. One even says to be careful with his sweet nectar he would still like her to be serviceable later, which prompted the twins to reply that nothing that black men pound will be of use for days, then high fiving each other as the women both climax in unison and they finish on both pair of tits. Wiping their huge black dicks across the ladies' lips, both pair. Ok ladies, which of you are next to have your pussies ravished and husbands needing to clean you up.

Dante and KyRel make their way over to the larger orange couch and KyRel spots his favorite, Syndrel, he tells her of the wager that was lost in the Blue room and that she is Dante's for the night.

Syndrel is fair skinned, brown, and reddish haired beauty of Hispanic and African and Irish descent from the Caribbean. "Follow me Dante if you want your winnings." She leaned in and whispered in Dante's ear.

"I ensure you will not be disappointed and will leave with a deal to your satisfaction." KyRel confesses to Dante.

Dante looks at KyRel and smiles.

"You are a man of your word my friend and I hope you enjoy holding your dick for a very long time."

"Hahaha, you enjoy yourself old friend, the time will come when I will have bested you and I will not be holding my dick too long over your face."

Dante gives a quick glance of anger before being brought back to the attention of Syndrel and conducting business in the loft of the Orange room.

The old friends appear to have hit a snag, and now Dante will make KyRel regret his words and put him in his place. He will bed Syndrel so well that not only will KyRel hear but the whole of the Orange room will come to watch and applaud.

No one will hold their dick over my face he is thinking as he bends Syndrel over the rail and slowly enters her driving his dick deep into her open wet pussy.

"Shall we commence negotiations, or shall this be a hostile takeover with your assets plundered and thoroughly depleted?" Dante says as he looks down at KyRel.

"Neither", Syndrel responds, as she quickly flips around and pushes Dante on the wall begins to locate his tiny balls and squeezes his erection till it erupts and he is left limp, and she walks back down to KyRel and kissing him long and hard, and they look up at Dante who is looking down on them with a look of disdain.

"Behold the great Dante York, the world's greatest lover. Even greater than Valentino! Reduced to a one pump chump and lasted less than a minute with one of our best lovers. Let us toast to his greatness."

He now will really have to part ways with KyRel and destroy him.

How dare he forgets who has helped him rise above his means and carried him to a lofty standing and turned him into a man with whom everyone wants to partner and conduct business with and made him a Member of the Den in good standing."

Conspiring with that filthy rat whore Syndrel to embarrass him in the Orange room is a slight that will not go unpunished.

Just as he makes his way to the door, the lurker who had been watching their every move makes its move.

An explosion rocks the building, a shadowy figure is seen hurriedly slashing its way around the club and then into the Den. Chaos and blood curdling screams are heard throughout and body parts lay strewn about.

Dante lays pinned beneath the loft and is bleeding profusely from his wounds, the lurker stands over him and he recognizes who it is.

"You! You were pronounced missing. Why have you done this?"

The lurker runs off in a flash, as KyRel goes and stands over the fallen former friend.

"I told you I would not hold my dick long old friend; this is last time you will ever hold me under your thumb and treat me as a lackey."

He unzips his pants and releases a satisfactory moan as Syndrel holds his dick, another deal and last deal of the Den has been completed with an acrimonious end to a long-standing friendship.

Just as the couple begin to gloat, the lurker attacks and slashes Syndrel splitting her body in two and sending blood splattering all over KyRel, who cannot believe what he just saw and then he is slashed open, and bowels rent asunder.

The Harrisons are running out the door, see what happens when you do things with white people the one says to the other. "I see what happens to dickhead white boys and you know who did this man", the other responds. "I also saw that one dude nut on the dying dude's face. Damn! That was cold and nasty."

"We must get out of here, quick, she will come for us soon. And I do not want to be a part of that, we're not ready yet".

As the building starts to collapse the police have arrived and managed to corral some of the survivors and have more questions than answers. The only thing that everyone agrees on is that a shadowy hairy snarling figure had appeared with another shadowy figure that seemed to be a woman.

"You have done well Marcus." A voice says from the dark parking ramp.

"But I did not get to meet Wellington", he responds.

"No, you let me get close to my first targets, those two pricks were a thorn in my side for years, embarrassing me at every turn to only try to take down my father's business and create an empire of their own. With your help I was able to sow discourse between them and get revenge for how Dante plastered my name around college because I would not let him sleep with me. Now that my father has shown me who and what I am and set me free I will take down all that have tried to destroy him or me. Dante and KyRel were only the beginning of my plans and first to feel my wrath."

Rose laughs manically, then waves and flips her hand towards Marcus.

"Go to your second mission and remember I will set your family free when all is done, fail me and the good Christians will die."

"I will obey as you command my lady."

On the news report, Wellington is talking to the camera and offering a reward to anyone who can identify the persons responsible for the chaos and devastation.

"As a leader in this city, I cannot let this type of thing go unpunished and will do everything I can to help the police."

Behind the scenes Wellington, the Mayor, the Chief of Police and some of the city council members and others that are Members of the Den are plotting to reopen the Den and this time be more selective of the location and add more security.

"I have not seen such a foul act since the days of old, but it possibly cannot be him." Wellington is thinking to himself. "I was there, he was destroyed, and his remains buried deep in caves in the 6 countries of the Balkans and among the mountains of the Carpathians, so he could never again wreak havoc among us."

He is mumbling to himself, but the Chief of Police hears him and dismisses it as the old man is having an episode after witnessing such traumatic events.

Rose is perched on a roof top, looking down on all the destruction and mayhem.

"That is correct Wellington, you destroyed my grandfather, but you did not destroy his family or our clan. I have my eyes on you and soon you will fall as my prey. And the Farkas name shall be restored, and our Empire will rise from the ashes like a fire bird."

Long gone is the Rose Farkas that was the virgin mentally unstable sex therapist, now in her place is the violent ruthless gang leader, the wolf is angry, hungry and on the prowl.

Chapter 2

After a couple of weeks since the explosion, Dante York is laid to rest in the big cemetery on the hill. The cemetery where the elite and wealthy of the city are interned, known to most as Wellington Hill. While KyRel and Syndrel are given nondescript generic empty coffins that are buried in the county graveyard outside of the city and other victims have been laid to rest in the city graveyard and some others at the cemetery over by the old Episcopal Church and a handful over at Mother Grace cemetery down from the Mount Sinai Temple and the Greater Temple of Solomon Baptist Church.

And in the heart of the city at Saint James of Cornette, the oldest cathedral in the city, Wellington is eulogizing his latest wife who was caught in the explosion and died from shrapnel from the explosion and falling debris that crushed her so badly that all her bones were turned to dust.

At the conclusion of the memorial, Wellington appeared on an interview with a local reporter and again vowed to find the killer and stated that there was a 2-million-dollar reward now. Then scuffs off to his limo and immediately berates the driver to get him the hell out of here, he hates the old cathedral but must always pay a visit for his cousin is now the Parish Priest.

Before he could leave, Marcus appears out of nowhere and the driver bumps him slightly, but enough to knock him over.

"GOOD GOD! You are a blithering idiot. Now I have another lawsuit to settle."

But Marcus jumps to his feet and looks to be ok, Wellington, exits his car and attends to him with all earnest sincerity.

"My dear fellow, are you ok?"

"Yes Sir, I am fine, just a bruise or 2. I am so glad that I ran into you. He says with a sly grin. Which in turns makes Wellington smile and laugh."

"How may I be of service young man?"

Marcus begins by introducing himself as Marcus Willoughby, Wellington cuts him off and nods knowingly and says that he knows his parents.

"I heard that they have been missing for a long time now, I can help you with that situation if you would like."

Marcus cannot believe his ears, and his luck, not only did he contact Wellington, but he can now make inroads with him by playing him against Rose. But little does he know that Wellington is not who he thinks he is, and neither does him or Rose knows of the person that Wellington is known to be around the world.

The two head off in the limo with Wellington making a call to his security team to give Marcus a hand in finding his family.

Meanwhile Rose is putting her plan into action, she is on her way to the Harrison mansion, but first she will stop at their business headquarters.

The Harrisons are the most influential black men in the city, not only street smart but highly educated, both hold PHD's in mathematics and master's degrees in business. They cut their teeth working for their grandfathers, Father Harrison was a real estate magnet and oil baron, Father Wood, their mother's father was head of a violent street gang The Black Palms and mafia member of the Lugano Syndicate. And both were rivals to Rose's father.

Both men helped mold who these men would become, ruthless businessmen with a Worldwide oil conglomerate and real estate investors around the world. The private business is trafficking of drugs and women. This is the business that Rose is interested in.

She makes her way into the building by posing as a reporter investigating the explosion. Once in she is stealthy and cunning and moves from floor to floor until she locates her target.

An unmanned computer in the twins' office has been left on and unlocked, she gathers all the information about the real daily business and the private business. Just as she is finishing a door opens and a familiar voice says that they are meeting someone later for drinks and then taking the rest of the week off.

She hides behind a huge plant and waits for the voice to come into view. A quick slash of the throat should remedy situation, but as luck would have it, the voice belongs to her old assistant. Not wanting to kill her former assistant. She quickly takes the woman from behind and uses a choke hold to render her immobile and knocked out long enough for Rose to make her escape.

But all is not as it seems; the whole thing has been caught on the security cameras and security has been dispatched to capture her.

The first wave of guards finds her on the 10th floor, and she wastes no time in tearing them apart, only 4 she thinks, this will be a cake walk, then more and more begin to arrive as she fights her way down to the first floor, utilizing martial arts and blades and a few handguns to overcome her foes. Tearing and ripping at them to get away. Finally, the last group contacts her on the rear of building before she can get to the exit through the facilities maintenance section.

They ready for the onslaught that they have been warned of. Rose steadies herself and Boom!

The explosion rocks the building and sends glass shattering and spewing across the complex. The guards go flying with bodies hurling into concrete and steel structures, bones shattering, and body parts being pierced from the shrapnel. But one survives and cannot believe her eyes, as she sees a beast running through the door and no sign of Rose in the area at all.

The twins have arrived and cannot figure out how she managed to defeat the numbers of security they had and how Rose vanished, and the beast appeared. They only think that she must be controlling this beast somehow and then it hits them that this is the same beast from the Den.

Somehow Rose has found a beast to do her dirty work and controls it with some type of power. That is how she defeated the security and killed mostly all of them.

Josh Harrison is fuming and ready to go to war, but James is keeping a cool head and tries to allay his brother's emotions.

"No need to be huff and puff, we have nothing to fear, she only got dummy files that I planted, the real files are safe. We must get ready for her now, but we will need Wellington and his other dickhead white boys."

"Yes, agreed, but what if we get the beast from her and use it against her."

"Good idea brother, that is what we will do."

While the brothers plot and scheme, news has spread throughout the city of the attack and how the beast has appeared once again, sending the public and the underworld criminals into a stir.

Rose has returned to her lair and plugs the drive into the computer and begins to peruse the data. She soon realizes that she has been duped. In a fit of rage, she sets the place on fire and leaves no trace of her ever being there.

Everything she has done till now has been fool proof, where did she go wrong? How did you get fooled? Now she must start over and figure out how to get to these cockroaches. But first she turns her attention back to Marcus, has he made any headway with Wellington she wonders. He has not checked in yet and that is causing her to stress and lose control.

When she loses control things go very bad and she cannot contain the fall out of the mess that is caused.

Her inner wolf is again hungry, but she must not let it consume her and lose focus, stay calm she says to herself, we will figure out a new plan and the city will be red from blood.

If only her mother was here to help her. But what good would that do her? She would probably try to bed Wellington or one of the Harrisons or worse yet Marcus.

Focus Rose, Focus.

Chapter 3

Around a few months later and with Rose laying low, everything seems to be getting back to normal around the city.

The Harrisons are doing business as usual and rebuilding their headquarters but keeping an eye for the beast and Rose.

Meanwhile the erst while Marcus has been on the move, hobnobbing around the city with Wellington and meeting the movers and shakers and leaders of the city as well as the underground crime lords. Growing ever closer to the city's real leader and richest man.

One day he gets a call.

"Marcus, my dear fellow, its Wellington, meet me at the club we have much to discuss."

Marcus is now elated, this is his moment, his chance to be rid of Rose and hitch his wagon to Wellington and become the 2nd most powerful person and eventually number 1 and neither of them would see it coming.

As he arrives at Wellington Meadows, he can't help to be impressed, not only was a cemetery and other things named for his new benefactor but now he is at an amazing 100-acre golf course and park.

He exits the car and is met by a military styled uniformed gentleman that escorts him to the club grounds and demands him to wait here for Mr. Garrison. Marcus is so taken in with the vast building and all its accoutrement that he has not noticed that Wellington has arrived and has called his name a few times to gain his attention.

"I bid you welcome my dear fellow; shall we take the grand tour? There is lots to behold and to unfold and now that you are full member you will have access to all before you."

Marcus begins to act like a giddy schoolgirl and wonders aloud how everything seems to be named for Wellington.

"Well, that is because of my maternal Great Great Great Grandfather whose surname was Wellington and lineage dates to the Wellingtons of England and yes that Wellington, the first Duke, the General as we now know of him."

Marcus is stunned with how freely Wellington is with his background, but when you are the richest man and have a historical figure in your family tree, why not be free. The old blue bloods often speak of their heritage as a badge of honor and throw it in your face to let you know that you are not one of them and they are better than you.

"Everything he touched became incorporated with his name as the dear fellow was wanting to leave an indelible mark upon this world and leave his legacy everlasting."

"And how is your lineage, my dear Marcus? Do you know where your parentage hails from?"

"Sadly, I do not, I was never told of such things as my parents were never too keen on sharing family details. Only sharing the faith was their only recourse in life. I dare to say that one day I might discover who I am and be of some use to this world and leave my legacy as well."

With this Wellington takes the young man to a corner bar, "order any cocktail you would like, and it is on me."

With drinks in hand, they travel through the gardens, with Marcus in awe at every turn and Wellington describing every plant and flower and their origins till they come to the club house.

"Here we are my dear Marcus, the crown of the whole lot. Here you will find everyone you should know and want to know and know about. And they shall want to know you as well."

All eyes turn towards the two men as they enter, and whispers begin to fly as another uniformed man comes to take their now empty cravats and signals to another to fetch two more cocktails for the gentlemen.

"Marcus, can I trust you? Or dare I say can I require of your trust and loyalty?"

"Why certainly Wellington. I will do my best to not let you down."

"That is what I thought you would say, so let us adjourn to the course, we have a meeting to attend."

Who is the meeting with Marcus begins to wonder but does not ask. As they board a cart and drive over a few hills the course comes into view, Marcus notices that a pair of men are waiting and tip their hats to Wellington. The men have also put bags containing the golf clubs out and ask if that is all and Wellington nods in agreement and slides each some folded paper bills.

They say thank you and walk towards a small shack on the course. One picks up a phone and says they are ready; you can approach now.

Marcus recognizes the men that are approaching in the cart, it is the black gentlemen he had seen running from the Den. What type of meeting could Wellington possibly have with these guys?

"Ah! Gentlemen, it is good to see you after such unfortunate events over the pasts few weeks and months."

"Stop playing Wellington, we are not here for the bullshit, save that for your new wife. Let's get down to business and who is this goofy looking white boy?"

"Tsk tsk, come now James."

"You heard my brother Wellington, put the bullshit on those plants and flowers. We are not talking until you tell us about this cornstarch ass motherfucker, James is patient, but I am not here to play games with your colonizer ass."

"Gentlemen, manners please. Business is business and we are here for that, there are no games being played. Marcus, these are the Harrison brothers, twins if you will. Joshua and James, they are the two men that control some of the cities drug trade as well as prostitution, while conducting legal business as real estate moguls and own several gas stations that use the petroleum from their oil company."

"We also have a rubber company and launching an auto manufacturing company soon too, you old decrepit man."

"Yeah, you dried up cornstalk bitch. Tell us who this flour dough white boy is and stop trying to get on our good side before I whack both of y'all with these nine irons. And leave holes in one."

"I see, well we off to a rousing start. Gentlemen, this is my new associate Marcus, you might know his parents the Willoughby family that were kidnapped, the same that are the ones that have tried to help your most loyal customers and workers."

Seeing the Harrison's faces starting to turn angrier, and Josh begins to pull out his gold plated nine millimeters, Marcus thinks quick on his feet.

"Wait, I have information that might make all of us a united team and more money."

'What the hell are you talking bout oatmeal milk?"

"Calm down Josh, let's hear him out."

"Yes, Marcus, what is this about dear fellow."

Now is the time, Marcus will turn his back on Rose and go to war with her. And the best part is that these guys will do all the dirty work and he does not have to lift a finger.

"The woman that attacked your building, her name is Rose, Rose Farkas."

"Ahh! I thought it could not be possible, but I see I was extremely remised, this is a definite bonus kismet of providence."

"I told you James! I knew it was her at the Den, this is the move we have been waiting for."

"No. We need to plan this out, Wellington you know her family. How do we go about this?"

"I was afraid of this situation, coming to light, but Marcus, how did you know about Rose?"

"That is what I wanted to talk to you about Wellington, I was helping her because she is the one who is holding my parents' hostage. She wants to take control of the city. And will not stop at nothing to get it.

She targeted Dante first, saying that he had wronged her and tried to kill her father. Then she wanted to take down these guys because of an old rivalry with their family. And finally, she was going to bring you down and destroy you, your family and friends did something to her family long ago that she thinks you need to suffer and watch your world burn and be torn apart. And you two, your families are old rivals. She just wants to take over your family empire."

Wellington seizes upon the opportunity and leaps in.

"The Farkas family is not one to be trifled with, her father disappeared from the city, and no one knows what has happened to him. And long ago in the old world we had a social group or a secret society if you will. Her grandfather was a member of the group, but he was not a very good member and we had to excommunicate him."

Wellington turns away from the group and then like he was having a moment of clarity, although he was already ahead of them. Turns back to Marcus and lays in a plan.

"My dear Marcus, I think it is time we recreate the social group, since you have been so forthcoming with this, I will leave you to find a brilliant suitable meeting place for us, Joshua and James I would like to form a united front if you gentlemen are so keen do so.”

The twins not knowing what to make of the Rose situation, agree to join with them.

“Josh, we need to get all the men we can get, you know this chick is not going to go away, and Wellington and his new lackey are talking in circles with the secret society stuff.”

“Yeah, I don’t trust those crackers as far as I can toss them. Is he talking about creating something like the Illuminate?”

“I don’t know, but I don’t like it. We should be ready for him to double cross us and take down that chick Rose.”

As they play their round of golf, none of the men are aware that Rose has been watching and listening to the conversation.

She had planted a hidden camera and microphone on Marcus’s glasses.

“Marcus, you dumb boy, I knew you would turn on me, you will soon pay for that. But first I will make your parents suffer and let the world know that I am coming for what is mine and restore the Farkas name to its rightful place in the underworld. Wellington is only leading you astray and setting you up for his own purposes. What he did to my grandfather will fail in comparison to what I do to him. Time to let the wolf hunt."

Chapter 4

A few weeks pass and Marcus has found a nice building in the city that houses a nice rock basement, the old place was used as a barracks during the revolution and then a naval launching port during the civil war and then a speak easy during prohibition. The type of place that is obscure and had secret doors that lead in and out to other areas of the city.

"Marcus, dear fellow, you have outdone yourself, I have forgotten about this place, so quaint and very secret. Reminds me of the old skull and bones days in university."

"I thought you would be pleased, there is one more thing Wellington, it has several rooms larger than the Den and no night club to get in the way."

"That was the best part my dear fellow, it was a cover for the Den, but this is better, we can have more security."

"What shall we call this new place then?"

"From hence forth this shall be known as the Hearth and Mug pub. We shall make a FaceSnap ad and be Photogram influencers."

Marcus laughs at Wellington's boomer slip up. Wellington ignores him and continues with his diatribe.

"And our special group we will call the Tops and Tails and or new secret society will be known as the Brick-and-Mortar society. We will take control of all the city and its criminal underground, nothing nor no one will stand our path. Those who oppose us will be properly dispatched of and others will learn to fear us."

Marcus' eyes widen as he sees the plan Wellington is laying forth.

"And what of Rose? What is the plan to take care of her and get my parents back?"

"All in due course my dear fellow, like I have said to you the Farkas family is not one to be trifled with, we let the Harrison twins do their part and if they manage to survive then all the better for us."

"I see, they will be weakened, and we could take over their portion."

"Not only that but also, they would be vulnerable to a leverage buyout of the real estate and oil companies."

Wellington ever the opportunist and conniving rat, is reeling Marcus in and beams at his mastermind tricks.

Later that night a news report comes on and Marcus is heartbroken and shattered. His father's head was found on the spiked fencing surrounding the old church in midtown. Stuffed in his mouth was a paper that had a map and the words: To find the rest of me look to the stars and travel to the place that houses the bones of legacy.

This was the work of Rose; how did she find out about his betrayal? This enforces his resolve to end her and pushes him to work with Wellington more and not just have them fight each other.

As he makes his way to the Willoughby mausoleum, he passes by a weird marker, it has an inscription that resembles something he had seen at Wellington's country club and at the Den. He begins to wonder what they mean, but then remembers he had to be focused on Rose, she has killed his father and needs to pay for her deeds.

"I see you, you foul whore of a bitch, you take me into your bed and then kidnap my parents forcing me to do your bidding. Now you have killed my father, for what? What have they done to you? You are a heartless bitch, and I will kill you."

"Ha! You think you can kill me you momma's boy. If you had followed my instructions at the Den we would not be here now. All you had to do was get close to Wellington and I could have destroyed him and his world."

"Shut up!! I will kill you bitch; how dare you use my parents in your war."

He pulls out a Mossberg shotgun and fires at Rose, missing narrowly and continues to shoot and reloads after 6 shots.

"You are a bad shot. My turn now."

Rose pulls her 9 mm and fires four shots hitting Marcus in the knees and the shoulders.

"You betrayed me momma's boy, I figured you were a weak little bitch, but you forced me to make you suffer."

She walks over to him lying in blood and takes a deep breath inhaling the smell of the fresh wounds. But strains herself to not kill him.

"You will remember this moment and do not forget that you have your mother left. Continue the job I gave you or she will die next."

"I hate you bitch! Go to hell!!!"

"I have been there; it is a lovely place to visit. Mmmm. Your blood tastes like fruit, what have you been eating?"

"Fuck you! I will kill you if you don't kill me now."

"Many have tried and failed, no longer am I scared little girl or a mentally messed up sex therapist that was hypersexual, take him to the hospital and dump him at the door."

Rose's men do as she commands and meet her at the lair. They tell her that Wellington was there like he knew what happened and was waiting for them.

"I called him. Now he can comfort his little pet, this will put them closer and make Wellington unfocused. We must prepare for what is to come next. Until then go feast my pack. You deserve it."

They do as she says and fan out across the city, beating people and taking what they want. Raping and pillaging and no one dares to stand in their way, even the police seem to be helpless as victims are reporting seeing a beast with a woman but cannot describe her or the men.

The city is being ran amuck and Rose is now happy and filled with blood lust. She wants to make a scene that would make the Harrisons and Wellington mad as hell. She goes to the Wellington Foundation and accosts every employee, men and women alike are being beating and ripped apart. Blood covers the walls and floors.

Next, she goes to the Harrisons' strip club, patrons and strippers alike run frantically but cannot escape the carnage. One stripper in a sparkly orange, barely covering her body, outfit stumbles over an arm that was shot off, looks up crying and is quickly decapitated. Rose smiles and seems to enjoy the mayhem. All that is left is pieces of bodies mixed with pieces of wildly colored material. So much body fluid has been dispensed that someone could be pregnant or catch a std or bathe in it.

War has been declared and no one is safe.

Chapter 5

Having been devastated by the attacks, Wellington is odds with what he should do, cannot let Rose go unchallenged and he cannot confront her right now as he does not have the number of men he needs and word from the old world has not arrived as to what he should do.

He presses forward with the pub and club, while planning his own Secret Society. To keep his mind off the Rose matter, he takes up with a new lady friend. He has always had an eye for the Lady Weatherton, now that her husband has passed, he woos her and makes plans to add her to his bed and her wealth to his and become the next Lord Weatherton.

Weeks after parading about the city, the couple go to see Marcus, Wellington has seen to his recovery and tries to keep him in good spirits.

"Hello dear fellow, I would like to introduce you to my fiancé Lady Weatherton."

"How do you do my Lady; I was not sure Wellington could be lured and trapped by such a beautiful and intelligent person such as yourself. A vision of a heavenly angel and grace. May the lord take my eyes now that I have seen all I need to in this world."

"Charmed Sir, my you do have the tongue of devil. I see why Wellington is so impressed with you and quite frankly I cannot wait for you be on your feet and back to being up to snuff."

She winks and nods knowingly at Marcus.

"Thank you, my Lady, I appreciate the well wishes. But there is something I must speak to Wellington about alone if you do not mind."

"I bid you adieu kind Sir. Ladies should never be in the business of gentlemen."

Lady Weatherton kisses Wellington on the lips, not long just enough to wet them and pats his face and takes her leave.

"Well, you sly dog! How did you land such a pretty lady like that?"

"It did not take much my dear fellow, when you are wealthy beyond rich the best way to stay in such form is to marry wealthy, the beauty is just a bonus. And she knows about the club and pub. She is very keen to participate."

"Ah! That was also a question I was going to ask, now with that out of the way how do we handle this other situation?"

"We'll get you into that mobile chair and down to the pub and we shall discuss the situation and more. Come dear fellow."

As the two head off to their new establishment, the Harrison twins are trying to recover from this latest round of battle with Rose. They have put a lot of money behind fighting her and now need to put more men together and show the hoods that they are still in control before they start to rise and try to take them down. Rose is not the only one that smells blood.

"I am tired of this bitch James; she keeps hitting us hard and what the fuck is with that beast she has? Who has a whole beast like the fairy tales?"

"It is not a fairy tale brother, it is a horror story, and we are the victims, the white victims that can't figure out how to run and do stupid things that get them killed. We need to hit back and hard."

"How do we do that without that skeleton Wellington and his cornstarch cracker?"

"I say we go old school and flood the streets with guns, pay the hood boys, and let them get some revenge and motivate them to take her over her gang and pay us tribute to protect them. We keep them in check while getting rid of that bitch."

"Yeah, that bitch needs to die. And the dog pound needs to catch her beast thing."

"First, we need to get some special attention to rest our nerves and get us refocused on the task."

"I am down for that; I know some special treats that will be willing to spend some time with the Harrisons."

"Say no more, James is ready to play. Hahahahaha. A smorgasbord of all ethnicities and no big bitches this time."

At the pub, Wellington and Marcus have arrived and the Hearth and Mug is full of patrons, all having a good time and enjoying the live band that is playing. They do not even notice the men enter and the staff is working diligently to ensure that all keep having a good and fun time.

"This is fantastic, I never dreamed it would look like this. We are going to be rich, well you will be richer."

"My dear Marcus, I dare say that you are the one to be rich, I am just a silent partner in this venture that has recouped all my investment."

This brightens Marcus' spirit, but he has no idea that Wellington is making him the fall guy when things go down and he will be left holding the bag. In fact, Wellington has named him the principal owner and filed all the paperwork in Marcus' name. And naming Lady Weatherton as secondary proprietor. So, all in all Wellington is left devoid of any responsibility and cannot be found to have any legal or otherwise connection to the place or things that happen in the building.

"Shall we venture to the lower half and peruse the local goings on and see if we have the right mix of culture?"

"Lead on my captain."

Wellington takes Marcus to a hidden door that opens into an elevator and has him put his hand on the wall. A biometric scanner takes his handprint, and an AI asks him to place his eye near the wall for a retinal scan, then the elevator proceeds to lower them to the lower level that houses the Tops and Tails. There are a few ways to enter but that is the private way for the owners.

"Well, this is indeed a sight to behold, you have transformed my vision into a masterpiece Wellington."

The hallway is lighted with special lights so can you see silhouettes but not true faces, to the left is door with a security team that mans a door and only those with the password and phrase are allowed to enter and are searched and an electronic body scan is performed. To the right is the same, and as the members proceed to enter a bar is lined along either side. Further down the hall are doors on either side that open into the new fun rooms. Each a theme for all sorts of debauchery and deviancy.

The first room is called the torture chamber, it is filled with an array of torture equipment. A stock with a naked man in it being paddled by a man dressed in leather. A rack is stretching a lady while her partner is inserting a huge toy into her labia. Yet another man is laying naked on a bed of nails while being whipped by a lady dressed in leather that only covers her somewhat, her breasts are out, and her ass is not covered by the crotchless panties she is wearing. And that is only a few things in the room.

Another room is called the champion's room. In this room there are pools of different fluids and liquids that the members wrestle each other in naked. The winner moves to the big pool in the middle of the room and the overall champion is crowned when everyone else has been forced to perform oral or penetrated. The champion is then celebrated with a shower and their choice of members to satisfy them.

And still further down the hall a door opens to a room that is white and filled with toys and cribs and ladies dressed as sexy nurses. This is the play pen. A room for those that like to be babies or have diaper play.

Marcus cannot believe what he is seeing. He has never been a part of anything like this, and he cannot wait to fulfil his every desire.

"Do not lose control of yourself dear fellow, we have more to see. By the way, your equipment still works of course?"

Marcus gives a Wellington a glancing look.

They enter a dark room with only light coming from tiny flashlights in the corners. Muscular men clad with shiny silver sarongs are serving the members as they feel every inch of them with hands and mouths. Some are being fed grapes, cherries and strawberries and teased with ostrich feathers. Others have their toes and feet licked or shoes sniffed. This is the fetish room.

"Do you remember the orange room?"

"I am afraid I never made my way into that room."

"This next room is like that; anything goes if all parties are in agreeance."

As they enter there are several members already enthralled and entangled with grunts and moans louder than some the music that is played. Arms and legs wrapped around each other like Christmas presents. Wellington pushes him towards the mounds of naked flesh letting him smell the musky odor of sexual activity.

Marcus is feeling aroused now and is barely able to contain himself. Wellington noticing the bulge form in Marcus' pants cannot resist the urge.

"Do you see anything you like dear fellow?"

"I do indeed, I think."

"I believe you do my dear fellow, that is a nice little tent you have formed there."

"Are you messing with me or is there something you need to tell me?"

Just as Marcus was about to complete his sentence, he hears familiar voices and is now frustrated and feeling inadequate.

"You bitches aint never been stuffed with a 14-inch dick, much less with two. Come on get those pussies damaged and sent home soaking wet after these super soakers fill you up."

The room goes silent, and all are now focused on the loud boorish man in the center of the room.

"That is right Josh, tell your husbands, boyfriends or whatever you have at home that the Harrison twins have that meat."

"Yeah James! They know we are firing like nuclear missiles. And those little Vienna sausages they are playing with not getting that thang hot and juicy. Get over here and give me that juicy fruit girl."

"Oh, how I hate these guys."

"Do not fret so dear fellow, there are plenty of choices and they can only take on so many. Maybe you will be happy with one after they are finished with her."

Marcus looks at Wellington with a disdain that would kill an alligator. He is trying to maintain a cool persona, but after being almost killed that was hard to do.

"I don't do sloppy seconds SIR!"

"Calm down dear fellow, it was only a little jovial poke from the back. Although the negroes were breed for this sort of thing. Savagely ravishing their women, why do you think white women want them. And a few white men."

"I could careless, it is not about ravishing, I like to fulfill my women with satisfaction that they should never go wanting."

"All women secretly want to be ravished dear fellow, it is not the size that counts but how you dominate mentally and physically. Those chaps talk of being monstrously oversized and how they vanquish the vulva, but do they really last long."

"I know how to satisfy and dominate; I was with Rose for months and I am not the virgin or weak little boy that you think I am."

The Harrison twins see them and saunter over to antagonize them further.

"Look James, old man skeleton and his cornstarch cracker are here. What you 2 bouts to do, buttermilk biscuits?"

"Easy Josh, I saw Wellington's new squeeze, she is a hot thang that even Prince would bang. And has lots of money too."

"You guys would ruin a wet dream, just go away, and stop acting like."

Josh interrupts him while putting his hand behind his back.

"Like what? Go ahead and say it cornstarch. You know you want to. And as soon as you do, I am on that ass like a lawn mower on grass."

"Joshua, please refrain from such vulgarities, no one is trying to call you anything but the neanderthal that you are."

"I perfectly intended to call them a pair of monkey's asses. Do not defend me Wellington, these guys are insufferable and make me sick. We never should have agreed to partner with them."

"Rest assured little man, we have not forgotten and better yet, we have a plan that is being put into action right now. With you in that chair I figured you would have learned your lesson from Rose, but you don't seem to catch on."

"James whatever do you mean?"

"Can it Wellington, we will run this town when this over. Matter of fact, it's go time."

Josh leaps across the chair and punches Marcus knocking him out of his mobile chair. James throws a right hook that connects with the side of Wellingtons face. An all-out brawl ensues with the Harrison twins getting the better of everyone.

"We told you whiteboys, we're not to be played with, Rose and her crew are being taken out by our boys too."

"Yeah, all your cauliflower heads getting busted open, and its only two of us, haha. Get some motherfuckers. Come here cornstarch, where you crawling to?"

Both twins are stomping and kicking Marcus, Wellington, seizes the opportunity to slink away and exits through the secret door. Bodies are flying all over and the Harrisons are relishing the fight.

"You whiteboys don't know nothing about fighting, here, read my shoe cornstarch. Beat these fools like egg batter brother. Oh, shit motherfucker! Looks like you on your own cornstarch, your boy Wellington left you hanging or should I say laying." Josh lets out a menacing laugh that would send a cold chill down a murderer's back.

"We should kill you, but we will leave you here to lick your wounds and let this be a reminder to never mess with the Harrisons again. Burn this place down Josh."

Everyone flees the building not stopping to help Marcus, just trying to escape to save themselves.

Across the city the hood boys are making their way into Rose's lair. In the upstairs room there is music playing, the Isley Brothers song Contagious. Rose is being licked from head to toe and fucked by two guys. Seemingly not to not notice that they are about to be interrupted.

Just as the hood boys open fire all hell breaks loose, and a pair of snarling beast grabs and slashes its way through them and then a crash through the window.

"Hello, Marius, I have been waiting for you?"

"No. It cannot possibly be, I had a thought, but you were pronounced missing, and you were killed, we killed you long ago. What is going on here? How is this possible?"

"You and your snobby friends did not finish the job; you forgot a very important part of the ritual."

"Enough talk, we must end this now, he is no match for all of us. Those guys the Harrisons sent are dead, and you want to take on this empty vessel. He will die soon enough let's finish those two off."

"No son, I only meant to say we should make Marius see what he has wrought. The new love of his life and his future."

"What have you done? How dare you evil miscreants challenge me. And stop calling me Marius. Marius is dead."

"Come now Marius, you of all people should know how this was to end. It was inevitable, you and your Secret Society thought you could rid the world of us, but you forgot about my son and the awakening of my granddaughter. And that we had a secret partner in all of this."

"Yes, I know all about Marcus and his dalliances with Rose, he was a fool and will meet his end soon enough."

"No, you incessant fool. We are talking about her."

In walks a giant beast, transforming into the beautiful Lady Weatherton. Wellington is aghast and falls to his knees.

"That is correct my dear fellow as you are prone to say, and now you know. The Farkas family is reunited, Daughter and Father, Father and Son and Husband and Wife, Grandmother and Granddaughter. Yes, WIFE! Laszlo and Dorottya, the everlasting love."

Wellington is replaying through his mind; how did he miss this. What part of the ritual was not complete? How did he not know of Laszlo's wife? How had she fooled him into thinking she was Lady Weatherton?

"Look how puzzled the great Wellington is? Or should I say the great Prince of the Carpathians."

"Stop Dorottya, he is embarrassed enough, let us leave him here and have those pesky twins kill him."

"Come Rose, let grandmother look upon you. I have so much to tell you of your family that your father did not tell you."

The family leaves but as they do so they did not notice that one of the hood boys was still alive and had seen everything. He calls the twins and informs them of what he has seen.

"Werewolves!!! Are you fucking joking man? This cannot be serious."

"I told you James, this is a fairy tale."

"No, Josh it is a horror story, and you know how that ends for black people."

Back at the lair, Wellington is still processing what has happened, he gets a call, all his assets are gone, his money, the golf club, and the estate. All transferred to Lady Weatherton.

And even more devastating, the call from the old world comes. He is being summoned to the castle to be put through the test of Mirrors, Doors and Paths. A test so devastating to those with the blood of vampires, only the strongest and most evil survive it. Will he defy them and remain or go and possibly be put to the stake.

His thoughts are broken by a thud, he looks to the corridor, but sees no one there. Again, a thud, he turns to a room not far from the stairs.

He opens the door and finds Mrs. Willoughby laying bound and gagged in a chair on her side. They had left the poor lady to die, forgotten and miserable. A thought forms in Wellington's mind. How splendid this would work for him.

"Hello, my dear lady, you must be Mrs. Willoughby? I am here to rescue you from the foul beastly ruffians."

"Who are you Sir?"

"I am Wellington Stetson McCoy Garrison the Fifth, I knew your son Marcus and promised him I would do all I could to see you free."

"What has happened to my son and my Husband? Where is my HUSBAND?"

"I am sorry dear lady, your son was killed by some men that are on their way here to kill me, we must leave at once."

"But what happened to my husband?"

"Let us away, I will tell you on the way."

Across the city the Farkas family in whole are arriving at the Hearth and Mug, to find it burnt to the ground, as they make their way around the premises, they come across a survivor.

Laszlo confronts the man while lifting him high in the air. "Who has done this thing?"

"It was two guys, twins, they killed the owner and beat everyone up, I hid here in the back and then they set the place on fire, I was trapped until you came and moved the door."

"Sniveling coward!"

"Father, it was the Harrisons, we should have destroyed them at their office." Rose Bellows.

"No, my child, we will need them later against Wellington." Laszlo realizing the implications and consequences they might have on the family and keeping a dark secret.

"Yes, grandfather. I understand."

"I found Marcus' body downstairs. Rose, take it to the new lair and prep it for the fight." Dorottya commands.

"Yes, Grandmother, I am sure his mother will be more than ready to join us after she hears about his death."

But little do the Farkas' know that Wellington has already found her and is trying to sway her to his side. And the Harrisons are weighing which side to join, the Werewolves or Wellington. They should kill Wellington, but how do you kill werewolves?

Chapter 6

A plane lands at the city Airport. It is all black with no signage or ID number. When the ground crew goes to check the plane over, they find no one on board and the interior of the plane is laid out with very few seats for a plane that size and report to the tower what they have found.

"Impossible! There must be a crew or someone on board."

"No one at all control, it is like they vanished."

"Get security and the police down there now, no one leaves that plane everyone stays where you are until they arrive."

Security checks the plane all over and searches the cameras to see if anyone has disembarked the aircraft. They find nothing. The flight data and logs are checked, and the only thing found is that the plane left Romania a week ago stopped in England and then arrived at the city airport.

The plane is taken to a hanger, locked in with armed security in and around the area. No one is permitted in without clearance.

A shadowy figure lurks in the shadows of the dark.

"Yes, the plane has been taken care of, we will not have any trouble when we are ready to leave. They will never know we were here at all."

"Careful, they have a sixth sense and telepathically can speak to each other. This is to be a tag and bag mission and if we take him out also, that would not be so bad either."

Who are these new players that have entered the fray? Who is the lurker in the dark? Why does Laszlo call Wellington Marius?

www.ingramcontent.com/pod-product-compliance
Lightning Source LLC
Chambersburg PA
CBHW060910130726
48001CB00006B/2185